THE EROTIC TEMPLE 2

A SEXY FAIRY TALE

CLOVER'S FANTASY ADVENTURES
BOOK 12

VICTORIA RUSH

VOLUME 12

CLOVER'S FANTASY ADVENTURES -
BOOK 12

COPYRIGHT

ALSO BY VICTORIA RUSH

Adult Fairytales:

The Enchanted Forest: An Erotic Fairytale

The Land of Giants: An Erotic Fairytale

The Dragon's Lair: An Erotic Fairytale

Witch's Brew: An Erotic Fairytale

The Mage's Spell: An Erotic Fairytale

The Mermaid Lagoon: An Erotic Fairytale

The Coven: An Erotic Fairytale

Rapunzel: An Erotic Fairytale

The Seven Dwarfs: An Erotic Fairytale

The Land of Mutants: An Erotic Fairytale

The Erotic Temple: A Sexy Fairytale (Coming Soon)

Erotica Themed Bundles:

Voyeur: Lesbian Erotica Bundle

Public Affairs: A Lesbian Anthology

Futa Fantasies: The Ladyboy Collection

Threesomes: The Lesbian Collection

Threesomes - Volume 2: The Lesbian Collection

First Time: A Lesbian Anthology

Hedonism: An Erotic Anthology

Switch Hitters: Bisexual Erotica

Taboo Erotica: The Lesbian Series

BDSM: The Lesbian Collection

Party Games: The Erotic Collection

Party Games 2: The Erotic Collection

All Girl 1: Lesbian Erotica Bundle

All Girl 2: Lesbian Erotica Bundle

All Girl 3: Lesbian Erotica Bundle

All Girl 4: Lesbian Erotica Bundle

Erotic Fairytale Bundles:

Clover's Fantasy Adventures: Books 1 - 5

Clover's Fantasy Adventures: Books 6 - 10

Erotic Fantasy:

Pirate's Bounty: A Time Travel Adventure

Wild West: A Time Travel Adventure

Private Riley: A Time Travel Adventure

Cleopatra's Secret: A Time Travel Adventure

Bounty Hunter 2125: A Time Travel Adventure

Ninja Assassin: A Time Travel Adventure

The 300: A Time Travel Adventure

Arabian Nights: An Erotic Fairytale (coming soon...)

Steamy Time Travel Bundles:

Riley's Time Travel Adventures: Books 1 - 5

Lesbian Erotica:

The Dinner Party: Lesbian Voyeur Erotica

The Darkroom: Bisexual Voyeur Erotica

Naked Yoga: Lesbian Transgender Erotica

Nude Cruise: Bisexual Voyeur Erotica

Rush Hour: Taboo Public Sex

The Girl Next Door: First Time Lesbian Erotic Romance

Girls' Camp: Lesbian Group Sex

Wet Dream: Ladyboy Fantasy Erotica

The Convent: Taboo Sex with a Nun

Sex Robot: A Dream Sex Machine

The Personal Trainer: Getting Pumped at the Gym

The Dominatrix: BDSM Lesbian Domination

Webcam Chat: Lesbian Online Sex

Paint Me: A Kinky Bodypainting Workshop

The Toy Party: Girls Sharing Sex Toys

The Costume Party: Strapping One On

Swedish Sauna: Lesbian Group Sex

The Therapist: Taboo Lesbian Erotica

Elevator Shaft: Bisexual Threesomes Erotica

Ladyboy: Lesbian Transgender Erotica

Peep Show: Lesbian Voyeur Erotica

The Dare: Public Sex Erotica

Maid Service: Lesbian Threesomes Erotica

The Hitchhiker: First Time Lesbian Erotica

The Housesitter: Spycam Lesbian Erotica

The Spa: Lesbian Group Orgy

Parlor Games: Blindfold Sex Party

The Exchange Student: First Time Lesbian Erotica

The Hostel: Bisexual Group Erotica

The Harem: Lesbian Erotic Romance

The Orient Express: Lesbian Voyeur Erotica

The First Lady: A Forbidden Lesbian Erotic Romance

The Slave: Lesbian BDSM Erotica

The Masseuse: Lesbian Sensuous Erotica

Too Close for Comfort: Lesbian Forbidden Erotica

Naked Twister: A Wild Party Game

Lexi: The Sex App (Lesbian Fantasy Erotica)

Call Girl: Lesbian Bisexual Threesomes Erotica

Circle Jill: Lesbian Masturbation Workshop

The Viewing Room: Masturbation Voyeur Erotica

Spin the Bottle: A Kinky Party Game

The Hair Salon: Lesbian Voyeur Erotica

Tribadism 1: Girls Only Sex Workshop

Tribadism 2: The Art of Scissoring

Tribadism 3: Threeway Hookups

The Kiss: A Game of Oral Sex

Pledge Week: Sorority Sisters

Carny Games 1: A Wild Sex Party

Carny Games 2: A Kinky Sex Party

Carny Games 3: An Erotic Sex Party

Dreamscape: An Artificial Reality Game

Glory Hole: Guess Who's On the Other Side

Joy Ride: A Late Night Erotic Bus Trip

The Blind Girl: An Erotic Romance(Coming Soon)

Lesbian Erotica Bundles:

Jade's Erotic Adventures: Books 1 - 5

Jade's Erotic Adventures: Books 6 - 10

Jade's Erotic Adventures: Books 11 - 15

Jade's Erotic Adventures: Books 16 - 20

Jade's Erotic Adventures: Books 21 - 25

Jade's Erotic Adventures: Books 26 - 30

Jade's Erotic Adventures: Books 31 - 35

Jade's Erotic Adventures: Books 36 - 40

Jade's Erotic Adventures: Books 41 - 45

Jade's Erotic Adventures: Books 46 - 50

Fifty Shades of Jade: Superbundle

Standalone Stories:

The Polynesian Girl: A Lesbian EroticRomance

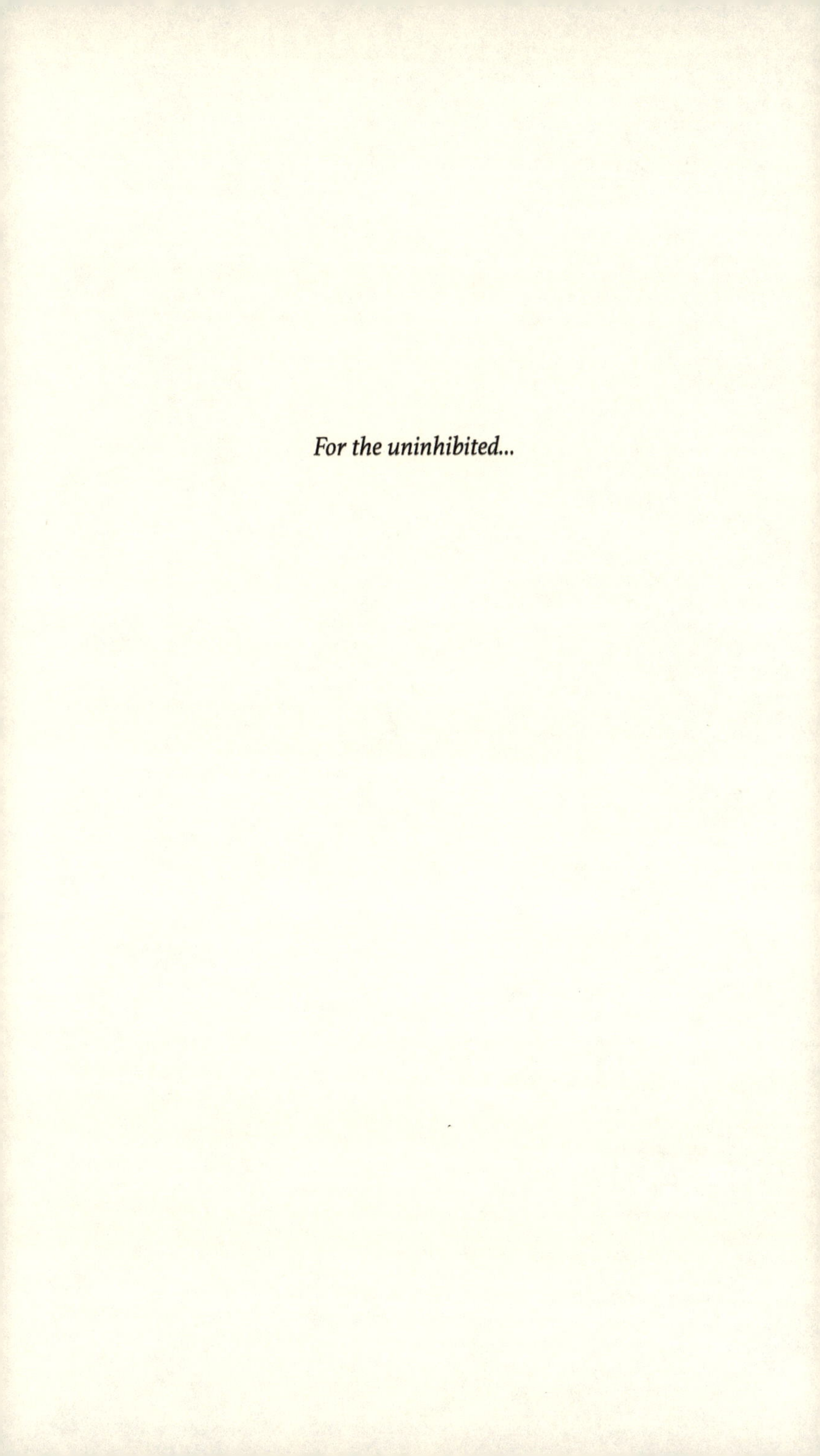

For the uninhibited...

WANT TO AMP UP YOUR SEX LIFE?

Sign up for my newsletter to receive more free books and other steamy stuff. Discover a hundred different ways to wet your whistle!

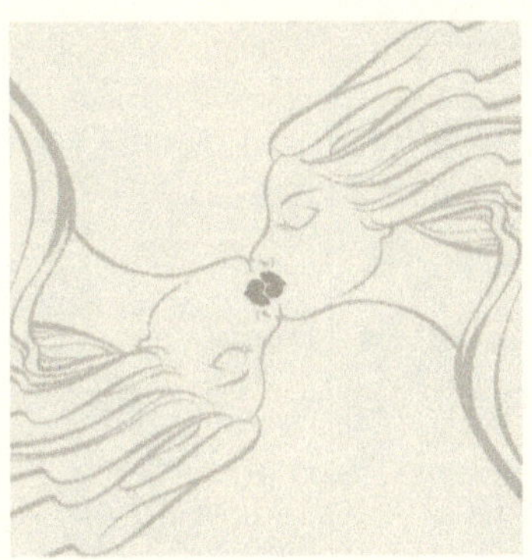

Victoria Rush Erotica

1

After Clover and Tara experienced their first fucking using their newly equipped cocks, they were eager to try other combinations to see what else they could do with their bi-functional organs.

"That last pairing was *insane*," Clover grinned, staring down at her still-swelling instrument, dripping a long string of cum while bobbing excitedly in front of her with each beat of her racing heart. "My dick's still tingling, what about yours?"

"Yeah," Tara nodded, rubbing the tip of her erect organ with her right hand while she fingered her dripping pussy with her other hand. "I thought most guys needed some recovery time after climaxing, but our tools seem to be already prepared for another go."

"What do you think, *Jessop*?" Clover said, peering over at her other friend, who was busy ogling the girls' big dicks while his own erection slapped against his stomach. "Your tool seems to be newly energized after that last pairing. Do you need a rest before we try to unlock some more of the natives?"

Jessop paused as he gazed down at his upturned cock with amazement.

"There's something about this place that makes me tingle," he said. "I could go at this all day. The possibilities with these tribespeople seem almost endless."

"Good," Clover said. "Because Tara and I are excited to see what else we can do with these oversize phalluses while we still have them. I don't know how much longer this magic spell will last."

"We've already tried them out on some *pussies*," Tara smiled. "Why don't we see if we can find some men to mix it up with this time?"

"Works for me," Clover nodded. "How about *you*, Jess? Are you getting tired of fucking other guys yet?"

"It's been a learning experience so far," Jessop chuckled. "Between getting butt-fucked for the first time and creaming over another guy's hard-on, I'm being stretched in ways I never imagined."

Clover smiled as she peered upwards towards the next tier of stone figures embedded in the temple walls.

"There's still plenty of other options to explore," she said, pointing toward another sculpture. "What about that one?"

Her friends glanced at a group of tribesmen standing with their butts facing one another while they each bent downwards, sucking their own upturned erections. Somehow, seeing them locked together in the act of self love made the scene seem even more erotic, and they quickly climbed up to the next level to begin stimulating their genitals. It didn't take long for the frozen figures to begin shaking and tremoring, and as their stone bodies started to soften and turn to muscle and sinew, the three tribesmen groaned as they pressed their mouths further down their swelling shafts.

"Fuck, that's hot!" Tara said, stepping back to savor the spectacle of the three men sucking their enormous cocks.

"No kidding," Clover said, gripping her hard-on with her right hand while she thrust three fingers of her other hand deep inside her sopping pussy. "I wonder what it feels like to get a blow-job from a man?"

"I dunno," Tara grinned, circling her dripping crown with the tips of her fingers. "But everyone says they do it better than women. I suppose they already know where the most sensitive parts are."

"What do you say, Jess?" Clover smiled, watching Jessop squeeze his balls while he watched the three men auto-fellating themselves. "Haven't you ever fantasized about getting sucked off by a guy?"

"Yeah," Jessop nodded. "Although in this case, I might be willing to switch positions for a change. I'd love to feel one of those guys' big tools in my mouth..."

"It doesn't look like we'll have to wait much longer," Tara chuckled, noticing the tribesmen's balls beginning to rise as their now fully animated organs throbbed in their mouths.

"Fuck, I need some of that," Clover nodded as she absent-mindedly stroked her own swelling organ.

Seconds later, the three men lowered their heads in tandem, until their lips touched the base of their balls as they wrapped their arms around the back of their knees, locking their bodies into a folded position while they squirted their seeds deep down their throats.

"Do you *see* that?" Clover said, watching their shafts pulsating with each contraction and spurt of their powerful orgasms.

"*Shit*, yes," Tara panted, stroking her cock ever faster. "That might be the hottest thing I've ever seen in my life."

"It's bringing back some memories," Jessop smiled as he

stared at the quivering trio of tribesmen while they throat-fucked themselves, happily drinking down every last drop of their spurting semen.

When they finally stopped shaking and quivering, they pulled their heads off their swelling tools and stood up, peering at the excited faces of their curious liberators.

"Thank you," each of them said, remembering how their leader had told them how they'd be eventually freed.

"Is there any way we can repay your kindness?" one of the tribesmen said.

"Well actually," Clover said, peering at their dripping erections. "We were kind of wondering what that felt like. You see, my friend and I have just recently grown one of our own. I don't suppose you'd like to—"

"We'd be happy to," the second tribesman said, glancing at the women's throbbing tools and glistening inner thighs. "But what about the *boy*?"

Jessop's grin stretched wide as a Cheshire Cat while he stared at the native man's beautiful pole.

"I was thinking of switching positions with you," he said. "I've never sucked another man's cock that big before."

"Are you sure you'll be able to fit me in your mouth?" the tribesman grinned. "It looks like you've been practicing on somewhat smaller appendages."

"Maybe not *all* of it," Jessop chuckled. "But I'm willing to give it a try."

"Alright then," the third tribesman said, striding toward Tara and dropping onto his knees in front of her flexing pecker. "It looks like all three of you are ready."

"Yessss," Tara groaned when the man took her erect tool in his mouth and began swirling his tongue around the sensitive flesh under the coronal ridge of her glans.

"Can I have some of that?" Clover said toward the second

native man as he kneeled in front of her upturned erection, staring at her quivering breasts.

"Mmm," he hummed, taking her dick into his mouth while he wrapped his hands around the back of her ass, squeezing her buttocks.

"Uh!" she inhaled sharply, surprised at how good it felt to feel a man's lips around her throbbing instrument.

"Feels incredible, doesn't it?" Tara nodded as she peered over at Clover's hard-on bobbing in and out of the other tribesman's mouth.

"Are you kidding me?" Clover panted. "Now I see why queer guys say once you go gay, there's no other way."

"What about you, Jess–" Tara began to say, stopping herself when she noticed Jessop's head already planted halfway down over the thick shaft of the third tribesman's prick.

"I don't think you should distract him right now," Clover smiled. "He seems to have other things on his mind at the moment."

"Not to mention stuffing his *face*," Tara chuckled, face-fucking her partner while he pressed his hands between her legs to caress her dripping vulva, slipping two of his fingers deep into her cavity.

"Oh my God," Clover huffed beside her as she felt the other tribesman slip one of his fingers between her ass checks to tickle her rosebud.

"I don't think this is the first time these guys have done this sort of thing before," Tara grunted, beginning to feel her pleasure building toward the bursting point.

"Yes," Clover panted while she arched her body forward over the back of her partner. "This feels a lot different than fucking a pussy..."

"I don't know if it's because of what they're doing with

their *tongues,* or the fact that we're fucking two *dudes* with our new cocks–"

"Right now, I could come with a *rooster* sucking my cock," Clover nodded as her buttocks began to quiver in anticipation of the flood of pleasure rising inside her pelvis. "I can't hold it much longer..."

"Fuck, yes," Tara groaned as she grabbed the back of her partner's head, pulling his lips all the way down the length of her throbbing erection. "I'm gonna gush my juices over this guy's face any second now."

Suddenly, the two women heard some loud grunting noises coming from Jessop's direction, and when they saw his partner tensing his buttocks in obvious climax while Jessop jetted his own semen upwards toward his shaking balls in uncontrolled excitement, they both tumbled over the edge in mutual pleasure.

"Uhnnn," Clover groaned as a deep flush rolled over her bouncing tits toward her face. *"Oh fuckkkkkk..."*

"Sssssssst," Tara hissed in unison, exhaling rapidly as she squirted her pussy juices all over her partner's face while her erection throbbed in his mouth.

"Mmmft," was all Jessop could murmur as the last tribesman emptied his seed in long, hard pulses down his throat while Jessop humped his hips blindly in the air, climaxing simultaneously without a single touch to his own quivering instrument.

While the three friends squealed and trembled in simultaneous pleasure, they barely even noticed the shifting gazes of the other embedded figures surrounding them on both sides.

2

―――

"That was hot!" Tara panted when she finally recovered from her powerful orgasm.

"No kidding," Clover smiled. "If that's what it feels like to get sucked off by a guy, I can see why so many gay men want to stick with their own kind."

"I might have picked up a few pointers for when the tables are turned the next time around," Tara nodded. "That thing he did with his tongue under the tip of my cock was insane. I almost came from that alone."

"Not to mention what he did with my *ass*," Clover said. "Who knew getting your butthole tickled at the same time would feel so good?"

"Don't forget about the *balls*," Jessop chimed in, wiping the last traces of his partner's cum from the sides of his mouth. "Guys really like to have their scrotum played with while they're getting their dick sucked."

Clover laughed at how quickly Jessop had embraced the idea of full-bore man-on-man sex.

"Exactly how much of that guy's organ were you able to

get in your mouth?" she asked while stroking her throbbing phallus.

"Pretty much *all* of it," Jessop grinned. "I'm learning how to relax my throat muscles to take it all in. Feeling his dick pulsing in my throat when he came was a huge turn-on."

"We could tell," Tara chuckled, glancing down at the pool of spent cum dribbling out of his still half-erect cock. "Do you think that thing's got enough energy left to give it another go? I'd kind of like to try mine out on some fresh *pussy* this time..."

Jessop glanced at the surrounding friezes on the temple wall beside them, then he squinted his eyes at a trio of women positioned in a triangle formation, each one licking the next one's vulva.

"Is it just me, or does it seem like those women are *staring* at us?" he said.

Clover and Tara peered in the direction of the erotic sculpture, then their eyes widened.

"Yeah," Clover said. "Maybe they were spying on us this whole time."

"And getting more turned on watching us being sucked off," Tara nodded.

"In that case," Jessop grinned. "Maybe they wouldn't mind returning the favor, since I was the odd man out last time."

Tara gazed at the sculpture more carefully, noticing the intricate detail of the naked figures. Their muscles and sex organs were so delicately carved, it almost looked like they were already alive, even frozen in their stone formations.

"Those pussies look seriously fuckable," she said as her new joystick began to harden and rise upward once again.

"No shit," Tara said. "Do you think they'd like some girl *cock* for a change of pace?"

"There's only one way to find out," Clover said, standing up and striding over to the sculpture with her erection swinging from side to side.

As she and her friends began to caress the women's genitals, the stone slowly began to soften and turn pink, with the three tribeswomen squirming and twisting their hips against their partners' faces. It didn't take long for them to begin moaning and rocking their bodies faster, until each of them erupted in a fountain of juices spraying out toward the shocked trio.

"Damn, that was hot," Tara said, spreading their slippery juices over her throbbing erection.

"I wouldn't mind some of that," Clover nodded, stroking her organ as she peered at the tribeswomen's dripping, pink vulvas.

"Who are you?" one of the newly awakened women said, pinching her eyebrows at Clover's and Tara's unusual genitals.

"Just passersby," Tara said, tilting her hips upward to display her now fully erect phallus in all its glory.

"Who chose not to pass by this strange and enticing temple," Clover smiled.

"And when we discovered how we could free your people from being frozen *in flagrante*, we couldn't help offering a hand," Jessop said.

"Not to mention a few *other* body parts," Tara chuckled.

"So we can see," the second tribeswoman said, widening her eyes at Tara's dripping organ.

"How would you like to try connecting with a woman a little more *directly* this time?" Clover said, turning her hips from side to side to slap her swelling phallus against the side of her thighs.

"That could be fun," the third native girl said, glancing

over at Jessop's sinewy body. "But how will we get your *boyfriend* in on the action?"

Clover paused as her eyes darted between the three figures of the native women and their own flapping erections.

"Well, there's three of you and three of us," she said. "Maybe if we link up in a chain, we can *all* have a little fun at the same time."

"We're used to that," the first native girl nodded. "How about if Faryn lies down while one of you fucks her in the standard position and another one sits on her face as she fucks the second of us doggy-style? Then the last one can face her getting a cream-pie while I eat your pussy from behind?"

"God, that sounds hot," Clover said as her dick bounced up and down, unconsciously agreeing. "Now we just need to figure out where each one of us will be positioned in the chain."

"Well," the second native girl smiled, noticing the rivers of lubrication running down the insides of Clover's and Tara's thighs from their throbbing slits. "Since we already know how to eat *pussy*, it kind of makes sense for you two ladyboys to be in the second and third position."

"That works for me," Tara nodded, eager to have her pussy licked while she fucked another woman. "Are you okay taking up the 'pole' position on the front end, Jessop?"

"If it means I get to watch each of you getting licked by a sexy native girl while you're plowing your dicks into their mouth and pussy, yeah," Jessop huffed, his dick now as hard as a rock and pressing firmly up against his stomach.

"Alright then," Clover smiled as a string of precum dripped out the tip of her throbbing cock while she pictured the kinky match-up. "Let's get into position and see which of us can come the fastest!"

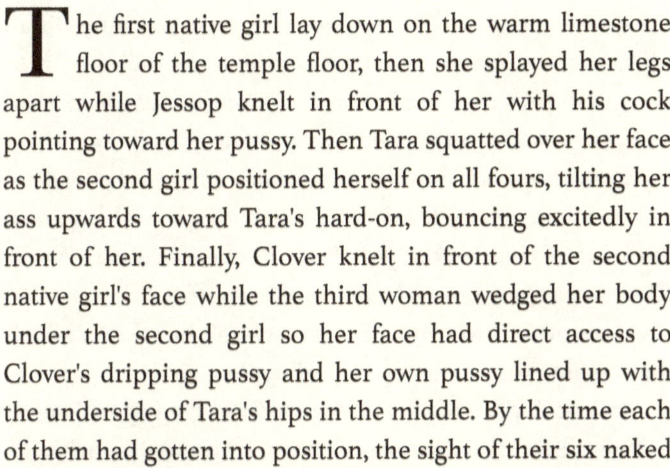

The first native girl lay down on the warm limestone floor of the temple floor, then she splayed her legs apart while Jessop knelt in front of her with his cock pointing toward her pussy. Then Tara squatted over her face as the second girl positioned herself on all fours, tilting her ass upwards toward Tara's hard-on, bouncing excitedly in front of her. Finally, Clover knelt in front of the second native girl's face while the third woman wedged her body under the second girl so her face had direct access to Clover's dripping pussy and her own pussy lined up with the underside of Tara's hips in the middle. By the time each of them had gotten into position, the sight of their six naked bodies dripping and throbbing next to one another was almost too pretty to interrupt.

But there was a limit to how long the three friends could stop to soak up the sight of their sexy sextet, and Jessop was the first to succumb to the temptation of dipping his cock into the waiting waters. As his erection sank into the wet folds of the first native girl's dripping pussy, he groaned and closed his eyes in heavenly bliss. As much as he'd enjoyed sucking the native man's big dick and climaxing together with him hands-free, there was never anything as good as the sensation of a woman's warm pussy. Especially one so pretty and lissome as the young native girl lying underneath him.

But his moment of blissful meditation was soon interrupted by the sound of Tara's groans as she lowered her aching pussy onto the waiting mouth of the first native girl while the second one pressed her ass backwards to take her flapping hard-on deep into her anal cavity. Tara's eyes flung open when she realized the tribeswoman had inserted her cock into her ass instead of her pussy, but when she heard the girl moaning and rocking her hips eagerly against Tara's hips, she realized it wasn't by accident. As they began to sway their hips together in tandem, Tara shuddered in pleasure, surprised at how pleasurable it felt to bury her newly equipped boy-cock into someone's back end. As she lowered her hands to the side of her partner's hips and began to buck her ass harder, the girl's body lurched forward, driving Clover's flapping organ deep into her mouth.

"Mmmft!" Clover huffed when she felt her dick slide all the way into the second native girl's gullet.

At first, it didn't feel so different from getting sucked off by the previous native man, but when the native girl lying underneath her raised her head and began to lick her dripping pussy at the same time, she threw her head back in ecstasy, panting loudly.

"How does it feel to get sucked off by a *woman* this time?" Tara smiled, watching the look of ecstasy spread over her face.

"You mean *two* women," Clover moaned. "I'd have to say it's at least twice as good. How about you? Are you enjoying fucking a *girl* this time around?"

"It could just as easily be a man," Tara grunted, digging her fingernails into the sides of the native girl's buttocks. "Since I'm taking her up the *ass*."

"No way!" Clover gasped, her eyes widening as she watched Tara's thick dick sliding in and out of the pretty girl's tight crack. "What does that feel like?"

"Kind of unexpected," Tara nodded. "It's tighter and smoother than you might imagine. Now I see why gay guys–"

"Never go back?" Clover chuckled.

"I suppose so," Tara smiled, enjoying the sound of her wet belly slapping off the cheeks of the hunched over native girl. "I can't wait to see what *other* configurations we can get into with these big pokers..."

"How about *you*, Jessop?" Clover said, glancing behind Tara at her other friend, who was pounding the prone native girl equally hard from the opposite end. "Are you enjoying this unusual hookup as much as we are?"

"Are you kidding me?" Jessop groaned. "I get a front-row seat to the best show in town, watching five women fucking and sucking each other while I have my way with yet another hot native girl."

"I only hope they're enjoying it as much as we are," Clover moaned, feeling the girl underneath her press her tongue into her snatch.

Tara noticed the girl wrap her legs around the hips of her friend, just in front of her thrusting organ.

"Judging by the *sounds* they're making," she nodded. "I have a feeling they're making the best of this new arrangement."

With the second and third native women's pussies now locked together by the grip of her scissored legs, they began to grind their vulvas together while the first girl continued eating Tara's cunt. Now that all six of the connected partners were positioned with direct stimulation of their erogenous zones, they soon began to moan more loudly together, building toward an explosive simultaneous climax. Tara had been trying to hold back her budding orgasm to make this new experience last as long as she could, but when she saw the juices jetting out of the two women's pussies underneath her, she lost all control and flew her head back, wailing in ecstasy as she buried her dick deep into her partner's pulsating anus, emptying her seed in long, hard pulses down the girl's tight hole.

When the second native girl's jaw clenched from her powerful climax, she unconsciously bit down on Clover's dick with her teeth, pinning her organ deep in her mouth. Instead of feeling pain as most men would when their dick had been bitten, this only heightened the feeling of pleasure for Clover, and she reveled in the sensation of her organ contracting in the native girl's mouth as her pole twitched and throbbed in her mouth.

For his part, Jessop had been so distracted watching his friends enjoy their sexy new connections that he almost lost track of what he was doing on the other end of the link-up. When he heard the girl lying beneath him moaning in plea-sure and her body beginning to shake in obvious climax, he leaned forward and squeezed her tits tightly as he pushed her legs forward and upward, humping her harder until he too howled in delirious pleasure, squirting his load deep inside her contracting pussy while he felt her juices squirting and sliding down over his throbbing balls.

Nobody wanted to separate from their partner's embrace for the longest time, savoring the feeling of their organs throbbing and dripping against one another, until they finally collapsed in a big pile together at the base of the tier. Jessop looked up and smiled when he saw all the gaps in the frescoes lining the lower tiers of the temple, realizing that he and his friends had been responsible for freeing a good number of native people already, all the while enjoying the fruits of their liberation in the most exotic and stimulating ways. Then he glanced over at his partners Clover and Tara and nodded.

"Do you think we're ever going to free all these people from their entombment?" he said, peering up the tall pyramid at the stacks of similarly embedded naked figures.

"What's your *hurry*?" Clover said, massaging the teeth marks left on her throbbing organ from the native girl that had just given her a blow job she'd never forget. "I could fuck these sexy native people for the rest of my life. Where else can you find your pick of willing partners who are ready to pair up with us in any combination we desire?"

"And where you get to play the part of the boy or the girl, however you choose?" Tara nodded, stroking her throbbing appendage like it was a lapdog.

"Who knows?" Clover grinned. "Maybe if you play your cards right, you *too* might become endowed with the organs of both sexes."

"No thanks," Jessop huffed. "I'm happy to keep my equipment just the way it is."

"Don't diss it before you *try* it," Tara chuckled. "You've already been pleasantly surprised by how good it feels to get screwed up the ass. Imagine what it would feel like if you had a *pussy* to match your impressive hard-on? The possibilities are endless."

Jessop paused as he reflected back on the sight of his two friends plowing their newfound tools into the eager orifices of the pretty native girls while they got their pussies sucked at the same time, then he suddenly felt a strange sensation tingling between his legs. As he peered down at his twitching organ, his balls began to shrivel and a cleft started to form under his perineum. While his eyes widened, two sets of puffy lips began to form where he once had a scrotum, and a distinct dribble of lubrication dripped out of his new aperture. But instead of being horrified by his unexpected transformation, his still fully-intact cock belied his excitement as it began to twitch and rise over his belly.

Now things were about to get really interesting, he thought.

3

______

essop was eager to try out his new equipment, so the three friends walked around the base of the second tier, searching for a pairing everybody could enjoy. After a few minutes, they noticed a lone couple, with the woman sitting on a man's lap while they kissed each other passionately. The tribesman's cock was deeply embedded in the woman's pussy, with her legs wrapped tightly around his waist.

"This one's got a little bit for all of us," Clover said.

"One man and one woman," Tara nodded. "We could take turns with each of them."

"Or have them *both* at the same time," Jessop smiled, his cock quickly rising to attention once again.

"Who wants to go *first*?" Clover said.

"Rock, papers, scissors?" Tara chuckled.

"Okay," Clover said, turning toward Tara. "Let's you and me try first."

The two girls clenched their right hands and pumped their fists rapidly up and down, finishing the last bob with open hands, Clover choosing scissors and Tara choosing paper.

"I win!" Clover squealed, then she motioned for Jessop to take his turn. "Now it's between Jess and me to see who'll sample the goods first."

The duo repeated the routine, this time with Clover choosing paper and Jessop choosing rock.

"You guys are so predictable," Clover laughed. "Watch and learn, kimosabe. Maybe you can pick up a few pointers as to how to use that pretty pussy of yours."

Jessop grunted in frustration, then the three friends walked over to the frozen sculpture to caress the two figures and awake them from their slumber. Within a few seconds, the man and the woman began to move and pant loudly, clasping on to each other tightly. When they shook their hips together in one final burst of passion, they moaned into each other's mouths then peered up at the strange newcomers who had just liberated them.

"Thank you," they panted in unison. "What can we do to repay your kindness?"

"Well, if you feel *up* to it..." Clover smiled. "Each of us would love to pair up with the two of you before you leave the temple."

"We'd be happy to oblige," the tribesman said, peering at the three friends' bisexual organs. "It looks like each of you could take us any way you desire. Who'd like to go first?"

"Me, please," Clover said, stepping toward the still-sitting couple. "Would you mind if I sat in your lap this time while your partner stimulates me from the other side?"

"That sounds like fun," the native man nodded. "Facing towards me or away?"

"Away," Clover grinned. "That way, the girl can rub her pussy against mine while you fuck me from behind."

"In your *yoni* up your *sphincter*?" the native man squinted.

"Yoni, please," Clover said, peering at Jessop. "I'm trying to teach my friend how to use his new boy-pussy."

"Assume the position then," the tribesman grinned. "I'm sure we can show him a few tips or two."

"I like the sound of that," Clover said, straddling the tribesman's midsection and turning away to face the pretty native girl.

She squatted down and pointed the end of the tribesman's thick prick towards her dripping opening, then she lowered herself slowly, savoring every inch of his huge organ as it sank into her hole.

"*God*, yes," she hissed, peering at the native girl as she knelt in front of Clover and pressed their bodies together. "Your breasts are so pretty."

"As are *you*," the native girl smiled, peering between their joined stomachs at Clover's swelling erection rubbing against the girl's furry mound. "Are you sure you don't want to point your tool somewhere a little *tighter* and *warmer*?"

"This is working just fine," Clover panted, beginning to rock her hips in unison with the tribesman behind her, who squeezed her tits tightly while he slapped his hips against her ass. "I want to watch my cum spurting all over your tits when I come. Why don't you rub your cunny against my hard-on to enjoy this position more fully?"

"Mmm," the girl nodded, wrapping her hands around the back of Clover's ass and pulling their bodies more closely together. "I've never seen a girl with a *totem* before..."

"If you play your cards right," Clover smiled, peering over at Tara. "You can try the next girl's cock up your *mitten* if you prefer."

"Yes," the native girl grunted, rocking her hips harder

against Clover's upturned cock while she pulled their bodies tighter. "But first, I want to watch your wand erupting between our bodies."

"It won't take long now," Clover huffed, sliding her breasts over the native girl's hardening nipples while she rocked her hips up and down over the tribesman's swelling erection. "Can you hold my cock when I come?"

"Yes," the native girl smiled, sliding her hands over the top of Clover's pelvis and gripping her poker with two hands. "Your pole is burning in my hands–"

"That's not the *only* thing it's going to do," Clover growled, feeling her rising orgasm approaching the tipping point. "Squeeze my dick hard."

The native girl glanced down at the crown of Clover's organ, which had begun to turn purple in her hands and squeezed it as hard as she could, as if trying to delay the inevitable eruption that was about to happen.

"I'm going to spray along with you," the girl huffed. "I can't stop it, this is way too hot–"

"Fuck yes," Clover grimaced, her face twisting into a contorted expression of unbridled pleasure as a sex flush spread rapidly over her tits, up toward her face. "Here it comes. Ungh–*gahhh!*"

When Clover's climax burst over her like a tidal wave, her cock spurted its semen upwards toward the girl's face, soaking her with a coating of white cum while she simultaneously squirted her pussy juices over the tribesman's tightening balls as he emptied his load deep inside her convulsing pussy. At the same time, the native girl tilted her hips upward, rocking her clit against Clover's pulsating erection, spraying her own juices over Clover's throbbing stomach, creating a symphony of juices like an undulating fountain.

Meanwhile, Jessop could only look on with his mouth agape as he gripped his throbbing hard-on with one hand and jerked three fingers of his other hand deep inside his dripping cavity.

"Holy shit!" he huffed, barely able to contain himself while he watched the threesome shaking their bodies together in the final throes of their mutual orgasm. "That was *insane*. I can't wait to see what it feels like to have my pussy filled up with one of those things."

"You might have to wait your turn," Tara grunted, squeezing the tip of her phallus in an attempt to forestall her own climax. "We still have to fight for who'll go next."

"Seriously?" Jessop huffed, tilting his head toward her in disbelief. "I don't know if I'm going to make it through another one of these hot match-ups before I spill my load."

"You'll just have to try to hold it in a little longer," Tara grinned, stepping toward Jessop and slapping her hard-on against the side of his as she positioned her right fist in front of his bobbing tool.

"I might have to pump this on something *else* if I lose this round," he grunted, beginning to rock his fist in unison with Tara.

4

———

Tara and Jessop shook their fists together three times, then on the last pump, they opened their fingers, with Jessop selecting paper and Tara choosing scissors.

"No fair!" Jessop complained. "You guys are reading my mind!"

"True," Tara grinned. "After you lost the last time to Clover's paper, I figured you'd steal her idea."

"Dammit!" Jessop huffed. "So I'm going to have to hold off climaxing once again, while I watch you having your way with these sexy natives?"

"Yes, but imagine all the new *ideas* you'll get for how you can use your new equipment," Tara chuckled. "You still have no idea how that new boy-pussy of yours works."

"I'm *beginning* to," Jessop said, dipping one finger into his slit as his hard-on bobbed excitedly against his stomach.

"Save that thought," Tara smiled, strolling over to the pretty native girl and the hung tribesman while her erect tool swung from side to side.

"How would you like to pair up with us *this* time?" the

native man said, his dick still standing straight up. "Your wish is our command."

"Well, I've already tried fucking and sucking with my new organ. I've always been turned on watching two guys rubbing their dicks together. I'd love to see what that feels like."

"My pleasure," the man smiled, spreading his legs apart as his erection bounced over his hips. "But what about my *partner*, how would you like her to participate in the action?"

Tara paused as she glanced over at the pretty native girl, watching a dribble of lubrication rolling down the inside of one of her thighs.

"I have a feeling she's just as excited as *I* am about the idea of frotting our dicks together. Do you think you can fit that tight pussy over *both* of our cocks at the same time?"

"I'd love to give it a try," the native girl smiled, staring at Tara's and the tribeman's twitching cocks. "Which way would you like me to *face*?"

"Towards me of course," Tara grinned. "I want to play with your tits while you squeeze our poles together with your wet pussy."

Tara lay in front of the native man's upturned pole, then she shimmied her hips forward until their two dicks touched.

"Mmm, it feels *hot*," she grunted, twisting her hips as she slid their throbbing poles together.

"So is *yours*," the tribesman nodded, examining Tara's girl-cock like he'd never seen one before.

Which, of course, he never had.

"Come," Tara said, motioning for the girl to sit overtop of their laps, facing in her direction. "Take your time, so you don't hurt yourself."

"I will," the native girl purred, kneeling down between

their legs and pulling their dicks together as she pointed their glistening tips toward her opening.

"Nnngh," she shuddered when she felt their combined crowns pressing inside her.

"Does it *hurt*?" Tara grunted, surprised how good it felt to have the girl's wet pussy surrounding their connected organs.

"No," the girl said, lowering her hips gently as their two cocks pressed deeper inside her cavity. "I just need to give it a moment to stretch and adjust to the thicker circumference."

"God, you're beautiful," Tara groaned, propping her arms behind her back so she could kiss the pretty girl and feel her tits pressing against her own. "This is even better with *two* cocks inside..."

"What does it feel like?" Clover asked, rubbing her tool with both hands while she tried to simulate the sensation.

"It's a lot *tighter*, that's for sure," Tara moaned, letting the girl do most of the work as she rocked her hips slowly up and down over the two swelling cocks. "There's something incredibly sexy about feeling another guy's dick rubbing up against mine. I can actually feel his *pulse* throbbing through his instrument."

"Fuck, that's hot," Clover shuddered, peering over at Jessop, who was stroking his hard-on in a similar manner as he stared at the intertwined trio. "Do you feel like giving it a try, Jessop?"

"What?" Jessop said, suddenly wrinkling his brow. "With you? How will we–?"

"We can hold our cocks together with our *hands*," Clover said. "It might not be as good as a pussy, but I'm intrigued to see what it feels like to frot another guy's cock."

"I've never done that with a girl before," Jessop nodded,

walking quickly over in Clover's direction. "This should be interesting..."

When the two friends came together, Clover placed her instrument atop Jessop's flexing pole, then they joined their hands around their combined hard-ons, rocking their hips together while they stared down at their darkening erections.

"So?" Tara said, glancing up at her panting friends as they humped their hips together between their tight hands. "What do you think?"

"You're *right*," Clover nodded as her eyes began to water from the pleasure spreading over her entire body. "This is crazy-hot doing this with another guy."

"How about you, Jessop?" Tara grinned, noticing her friend's balls beginning to tighten around the base of his dick. "Are you enjoying it as much as Clover?"

"Fuck, yes," Jessop rasped, dipping the tip of his organ into Clover's slit with every thrust of his hips. "This gives an entire new meaning to the idea of jerking off."

"Don't get *too* carried away," Tara chuckled, watching her friends' mouths beginning to gape open as their chests flushed a deep shade of red. "I'd hate for you to sap all your energy before you have your turn with our sexy new friends."

"Don't worry about me," he huffed, peering over at the pretty native girl, who had somehow managed to lower her dripping twat all the way down over her partners' swelling dicks. "I've got plenty in reserve for the next round."

Tara returned her attention to her partners, beginning to feel the familiar pressure of a budding climax building deep within her hips. She pressed her dripping folds down harder over the base of the tribesman's dick, feeling his balls sliding over her lips. The combined sensation of having her dick pressed against his throbbing pole while the girl squeezed them with her tight, wet sheath was too much to resist.

"I'm going to come any moment now," she hissed, taking one of the girl's nipples into her mouth. "Are you almost ready?"

"God, yes," the native girl panted, wrapping her arms around the back of Tara's head and pulling her tighter against her body. "I can feel it coming. I want to feel both of you shooting inside me."

When Tara felt the girl's hips quivering over their tools and she began spraying her juices against her belly, the native man on the other side suddenly groaned, grabbing the sides of the girl's ass and digging his nails deep into her flesh. Tara could feel his pole pulsing against hers, and seconds later, her entire lower body began flexing in powerful contractions, all the way from the depths of her pussy, to the entire length of her pulsating erection. But this time, she could feel every pulse of her dick as her semen shot rapidly through her pole, splattering the insides of the native girl's flexing pussy while she buried her head in the girl's chest, sucking her teat so hard it practically fell off.

Meanwhile, Clover and Jessop, who had been watching the erotic scene while they humped their dicks together, momentarily lost sight of what they were doing, spurting their cum against one another's belly and pussy, screaming in mutual delight with the rest of the group. When they finished ejecting their seed, they slumped together over each other's shoulder, panting heavily while they gripped their swelling dicks with both hands.

5

————————

"Holy *fuck*," Jessop gasped when he and Clover finally extricated themselves from one another's grip, staring down at their crimson poles dripping long strings of cum down onto the temple floor. "That was crazy!"

"No shit," Clover said, lifting a sample of her dripping semen up to her lips with one finger and tasting it approvingly. "Yet another reason why some guys never have the desire to mix it up with women."

"I dunno," Tara said, peering up at the flushed face of the native girl, who was still panting from her powerful orgasm. "I think you'll find it's even better with a warm *pussy* stroking your dicks than just your hands. There's something to be said for the soft touch of a woman and the feeling of her coming over your spurting dick..."

"What do you think, Jessop?" Clover said, peering down at her friend's erection, which was showing no sign of flagging, despite his recent orgasm. "Are you ready for some fresh pussy for a change of pace?"

"I guess so," he said, glancing down at the native girl's snatch, dripping long strings of cum from the combined loads of the two cocks. "But I'm even more interested in seeing what it feels like to be fucked by a *guy* in my new hole."

Tara peered at the native man, whose cock was still bobbing and flexing over his stomach while he stared at Jessop's glistening boy-pussy.

"Something tells me that our hung tribesman will be more than happy to oblige," she smiled. "Would you like to fuck the native girl at the same time? It's a singular pleasure coming from both *sides* at the same time."

"You're twisting my arm," Jessop chuckled, running his eyes over the girl's slim and taut body. "Assuming she's not hurting too much from the last pounding..."

"It's the least we can do to repay you for freeing us from bondage," the girl nodded. "One cock will be a lot easier to manage than two."

"That just leaves the matter of the *configuration* then," Clover smiled. "How exactly do you want to combine the three of you together?"

Jessop hesitated for a moment while he glanced at the tribesman's huge cock, then he glanced back at the native girl's figure, feeling his dick twitch as he stared at her tight, round ass.

"I'd have more *control* sitting on the man's hips, but then I wouldn't be able to enjoy the girl's body as fully as I might. Maybe another daisy-chain–"

"With the man behind and the girl in front?" Tara said.

"Exactly," Jessop nodded as another string of semen oozed out the tip of his instrument while he imagined the combination.

"Standing, sitting, or lying down?" Clover asked. "It could work in either position."

"Standing, I think," Jessop said. "I'll feel a little safer on my own two feet. Just in case this guy's a little too much for me..."

"Have it your way," Tara smiled, standing up and moving off to the side to join Clover to watch the next round unfold. "It looks like *both* of your partners are ready to go."

"Okay," Jessop said, stepping behind the pretty native girl and placing his hands on the sides of her curvy hips.

The tribesman followed suit, stepping behind Jessop's back end, and when Jessop felt his poker probing against his cheeks, for a moment he wondered if the tribesman planned to fuck him up the ass instead of his newly formed girl-pussy.

"You might want to bend over a bit more," Tara chuckled, noticing Jessop's eyes widening. "Just to make sure he finds the right hole this time."

Jessop bent down at the waist, and when the native man saw the pink folds of his glistening pussy, he wasted no time inserting his tool into his opening. When he pushed his hips forward, Jessop's own dick sank into the girl's hole, causing her to grunt in surprise. It had all happened a little faster than he would have liked, preferring to take his time to savor the sensation of the man's dick slowly penetrating his pussy and his own cock probing the wet depths of the girl's sex. But the feeling of the tribesman's dick inside his cavity was not disagreeable, and he soon got into a rhythm with the man as their three connected bodies rocked back and forth from the movement of the man in the rear. Jessop felt like the odd man out, wedged as he was between the two rocking bodies and having no way to control the movement of the larger tribesman standing behind him. Suddenly, he wished he'd chosen the sitting position instead, but the feeling of his throbbing cock moving in and out of the pretty girl's pussy soon distracted him from his thoughts of submission.

"What do you think?" Tara teased him from the sidelines. "How does it feel to get fucked like a *woman* for a change?"

"It's strange," Jessop grunted, feeling his body being tossed forward and back by the larger tribesman. "I usually prefer being in the driver's seat–"

"You better suck it up and enjoy it while it lasts," Clover chuckled, noticing the tribesman gripping the sides of Jessop's ass with both hands and pumping his dick harder into his cavity. "Because I don't think your partner has any intention of letting go."

"So it would seem," Jessop huffed, loosening his own grip on the native girl's butt in an attempt to soften the pounding that he was indirectly giving her. Suddenly, he felt a new sense of compassion for all the women whom he'd previously taken for granted, assuming they were enjoying their union as much as he was while he pounded her pussy thoughtlessly.

"It's a different feeling, hooking up with a *man*, isn't it?" Tara said, noticing the face of the native girl grimacing as her body lurched forward and back from the force of the tribesman's thrusting in the rear. "Sometimes you just have to go with the flow and let him take the lead."

"Try to focus more on your *cock*," Clover nodded, sensing Jessop's frustration as the native man probed him ever harder, like a stuck pig. "That should be something you can relate to a little better. Not every woman can orgasm just from vaginal stimulation."

Jessop nodded his head silently, realizing for the first time why some women preferred to have sex with their own kind, where they could take their time exploring each other's bodies and stimulating their erogenous zones directly without the distraction of a penis getting in the way. He vowed from that moment on to be more gentle with his partners and focus at least as much on their pleasure as his own, without relying only his dick to do most of the work. But it was a little beyond that point under the present circumstances, as the tribesman's increasing grunting from behind indicated he was close to reaching his peak, and he had no intention of slowing down until he was fully satisfied. Jessop winced as he felt the tip of the man's thick pole smashing against the end of his cavity, and he gripped the girl's hips hard to keep their bodies a distance apart to prevent her suffering the same indignity. When he finally felt the man groaning in climax as he held Jessop's ass tightly against his stomach, Jessop vowed to make his subsequent hookups more satisfying for his partners.

When the trio finally separated their bodies from one another, Clover and Tara glanced into Jessop's eyes, nodding in sympathy. As much as they hated to see their friend taken advantage of so roughly, they knew that Jessop would be a better man for having experienced sex from a female perspective.

"Time to take a break?" Tara said to Jessop, noticing his dick drooping in disinterest after his pounding at the hands of the hung native man.

"Yeah," Jessop frowned, glancing at his friends' flaccid tools, realizing they hadn't enjoyed the last encounter any more than he or the native girl had. "I think I need a moment to collect my thoughts, not to mention my *libido*."

"Don't worry," Tara said, stroking his flagging cock softly. "You'll get back in the swing of things soon enough. You just need a few more *girls* in the equation. Lord knows, there's enough of them remaining to be taken in this erotic temple."

"Yeah, well," Jessop frowned, stepping down from the temple's second level to begin exploring the forest for lunch. "I plan on doing a lot more *giving* than taking from now on."

6

———

Clover and Tara suggested hunting for some rabbits or wild boar for lunch, but Jessop wasn't in the mood for killing anything, so the three friends gathered some berries and fruit then sat near the base of the temple, peering up at their handiwork.

"We're beginning to make some progress," Clover said, counting the gaps in the walls where they'd already freed some of the natives.

"Yes," Tara nodded, glancing upward. "We've emptied the entire first tier and half of the second."

"It's strange how they ended up getting locked this way in the act of congress," Jessop said, nibbling his berries slowly. "It seems kind of cruel to freeze them in the middle of the act."

"Something about protecting them from their own destructive practices, apparently," Clover said.

"Well, they *do* seem pretty unrestrained in certain ways," Jessop nodded.

"I wonder where their so-called *king* is, anyway?" Tara said, peering up at the tall pyramid.

"How would we even know what he looks like?" Clover said.

"Presumably he'd have some special ornamentation," Jessop said. "Or perhaps he'll be a little *bigger* than the others..."

"It's hard to imagine them much bigger than they already are," Clover chuckled. "I don't think I could handle a prick much larger than these tribesmen have."

"Perhaps he's sitting closer to the *top* of the tower," Tara said, glancing toward the narrowing peak of the pyramid.

"I suppose we won't know until we get there," Jessop nodded, swallowing the last of his berries.

"Are you feeling ready for the next step in our adventure?" Clover said, glancing down at her friend's moribund member.

"I suppose so," Jessop said. "But this time, I'd prefer some *one-on-one* time with one of the tribeswomen."

"I'm sure that can be arranged," Clover smiled as she stood up, eager to get Jessop back in the game. "Let's see if we can't finish the second tier at least today."

The trio climbed back up the temple wall and walked around the perimeter of the next level, examining the remaining sculptures locked in intimate embraces. When Jessop noticed a trio of women in a new configuration, he stopped and tilted his head, considering how they could pair up.

"Hmm," Tara said, moving next to Jessop and glancing at the depiction of two native women scissoring each other with split legs while a third woman looked on, rubbing her own genitals. "It looks like somebody could use an extra hand. Or *cock*."

"Those other two appear busy enough," Clover nodded, noticing Jessop's cock suddenly twitching with renewed interest. "Do you think you can keep this single one distracted while Tara and I join up with the others, Jessop?"

"I might be able to think of something," Jessop grinned.

"Let's get started then," Clover said, moving closer to the sculpture and slipping her hand over the two native women's connected vulvas.

When Tara joined Clover stimulating the two women, Jessop walked slowly over toward the other woman, running his fingers softly over her parted mouth. It was a departure for him to take such an interest in parts of the native women's anatomy beyond their reproductive organs, and as he continued to gently caress her hair and shoulders, his two friends paused their stimulation of the tribbing couple to watch Jessop sensuously stroke his new partner. As he slid the back of his hand slowly down the native woman's arm toward her moving right hand, they nodded approvingly, rolling their hips together in unison.

"Damn," Tara whispered in Clover's ear. "I think something happened to Jessop after that last hookup. He seems to have entirely adjusted his approach to fucking women."

"Yes," Clover said. "He doesn't seem nearly in as much of a hurry to get down to business."

"It's turning me on just *watching* him," Tara nodded. "I wish more of the men I hooked up with took their time to get me in the mood half as well as he is."

"You're not the *only* one apparently getting turned on," Clover smiled, noticing the figure of the lonely girl beginning to rumble and moan as Jessop stroked her skin.

He slid his hand overtop of hers and fluttered his fingers over her moistening vulva, interlacing them between hers while she rubbed her pussy harder as her skin turned a ruddy pink and her writhing body began to separate from the wall. Jessop moved closer to hold her body, then the girl looked up in surprise, lifting her chin to kiss him passionately on the lips. As her body began to quiver and shake in the throes of climax, Jessop held her tightly, running his fingers through her hair.

When she finished shaking in Jessop's arms, his two friends peered at him in shock.

"Holy shit, Jessop," Clover said, rubbing her pussy unconsciously. "Where have you been all my life? You never touched *me* like that."

"Yeah, well, these native people are teaching me a few things," Jessop said. "Not the least of which is how to properly treat a lady."

"Well, I think that lady is ready for some *more* of your attention," Clover nodded, watching the native girl rubbing her body against Jessop's swelling dick. "Why don't you two take a private moment while we wake these other women and see if they'd like a couple more pussies to play with?"

"Good idea," Jessop said, peering into the native girl's eyes and clasping her hand gently to lead her to the other side of the tier.

As he and the girl moved away, Clover and Tara resumed their stimulation of the scissoring couple, concentrating their efforts on their dripping vulvas in an effort to wake them as quickly as they could. As much as they'd admired Jessop's slow and sensuous approach to wakening the other native girl, they were far too aroused after watching him to defer their own gratification much longer. After a few seconds, the tribbing pair's bodies began to twist and rock in unison as they joined hands, mashing their pussies together while their mouths gaped open. When they started convulsing their hips together in beautiful agony, Clover and Tara retracted their fingers, enjoying the women's climax while they trilled their swelling clits slowly.

"Damn, that was hot," Tara said, sliding her fingers up the front of her stomach and tasting her juices. "How can *we* get a piece of that action?"

"The obvious way would be for us to pair up with them separately and repeat the process," Clover nodded. "But I've got an idea how we can all please each of us at the same time..."

"That sounds a lot more interesting," Tara said. "What did you have in mind?"

Clover paused for a moment while she examined the base of the tier to see if there was enough room for what she was considering.

"I was thinking we could like down in a circle, joining end-to-end and facing one another. That way, we could each suck one of the other's pussy while we simultaneously watch the others getting stimulated."

"Damn, girl," Tara said, feeling a dribble of lubrication sliding out of her throbbing slit. "It looks like you're not the *only* one who's picked up a few pointers from watching these natives do their thing."

"As have *we*," one of the tribeswomen interrupted, glancing up at the newcomers' ladyboy figures.

"We'd love to suck your *cocks* while you eat our pussies," the second native girl nodded.

"God, yes," Tara hissed, her organ instantly bouncing up in front of her stomach. "We haven't tried *that* yet."

"Let's stagger our positions," Clover said, wedging between the two native women with her head pointed toward one of their pussies and her crotch toward the other's face.

The two native women separated their bodies until they were positioned in a semi-circle with only one link remaining to be filled, and Tara wasted no time filling in the remaining space, forming a perfect circle of curled bodies, joined face-to-crotch. While Clover and Tara buried their faces in the girls' dripping pussies, the native women seemed far more interested in playing with the newcomer's flapping *dildos* than their glistening slits. When they wrapped their mouths around Clover's and Tara's hard-ons and swallowed them whole, the two friends groaned loudly, sucking the native women's swelling clits into their mouths, sucking them equally hard.

As the group lost themselves in their own circle jerk, rocking their hips in unison and moaning together in blissful union, a few meters away on the other end of the temple tier, Jessop was taking his time to acquaint himself with the third native girl.

"What's your name?" he said to the pretty girl.

"Talia, what's yours?"

"Jessop."

"I like that," the native girl smiled. "How did you manage to find our lost tribe?"

"My friends and I were just traveling through the forest, not looking for anything in particular," Jessop said. "It was a pleasant surprise when we stumbled upon your temple."

"For *both* of us, it would seem," the girl smiled.

"You appeared to be enjoying yourself, watching the other women," Jessop nodded.

"It was a bit difficult wedging myself into the action with three yonis between us," the girl frowned. "So I decided to watch, instead."

Jessop turned his head in the direction of Clover and Tara, listening to the moans of the connected foursome.

"It seems that my friends have figured out a way to make it work," he chuckled.

"It's easier when they've got some extra *pokers* to work

with," the girl said, peering down at Jessop's swelling erection. "What can I do to repay your kindness?"

"I'd be far more interested in learning how to please *you*," Jessop smiled, sliding the back of his hand softly over the top of the girl's breasts.

"You seem to already know how to please a woman," the girl shuddered, her aureoles beginning to pucker as her nipples hardened. "Just keep doing what you're doing."

"Mmm," Jessop hummed as the tips of his fingers flitted softly over the girl's erect teats. "You have beautiful breasts, Talia. I love the color of your skin."

"Thank you," the girl panted as her hand drifted slowly down Jessop's abdomen toward his twitching cock. "Yours too."

Jessop shuffled his body a few inches away from the girl, kissing his way down her neck and circling her nipples with the tip of his tongue, flicking them softly as she moaned and purred in his ear. He was determined to focus his energy on his partner this time, trying to learn how to control his own urges while concentrating on how to better satisfy a woman. As he continued nibbling his way down her stomach, he alternately kissed and licked her, stopping at her navel to softly insert his tongue and tease her with a taste of what was yet to come.

"You're driving me crazy," the native girl huffed, trying to pull his head further down toward her throbbing pussy.

"In a good way or a bad way?" Jessop paused as a grin slowly spread on his face.

"*Both,*" the girl said, curling her fingers tightly in his hair. "It feels incredible what you're doing, but my nether regions are dying for similar attention."

"I'm getting there," Jessop murmured, shifting his head slightly lower to bury his face in her bush and breathe in the scent of her fragrant sex. "You smell so good, I could do this all day."

"Please..." the native girl begged. "I need you to suck on my pearl. I'm going to burst if you don't touch me down there soon."

"Mmm," Jessop hummed, feeling his dick becoming as hard as a rock. "How would you like me to do it exactly? I mean, in which position..."

"Can I sit on your *face*?" the girl said, shifting up onto her knees. "I want to watch you while you're licking my pussy."

"It would be my pleasure," Jessop said. "In which direction would you like to face–forward or away?"

The native girl hesitated as she glanced down at Jessop's flapping erection, licking her lips while a smile spread over her face.

"Towards your *cock*," she said. "I want to see you getting turned on while you suck my yoni."

"There's no doubt about that," Jessop chuckled. "I'm already as turned on as I could possibly be, worshipping your gorgeous body."

"Well, let's do some worshipping *together* while you lap up my juices," the girl said as Jessop flipped onto his back and she lowered her face onto his waiting hips.

When he felt her wet folds pressing down over his face, he nibbled her labia, sliding his tongue along the inside of her cleft until he reached the point where they joined together over her hardening button. Instead of inhaling it immediately, as he was accustomed, he teased her instead, kissing and nibbling on it softly while he licked around the perimeter, drinking down her juices as she flooded his mouth.

"You're not like most men," the girl groaned, mashing her hips harder onto Jessop's face. "I like the way you tease me and build the anticipation. I'm going to come even harder when you take me into your mouth."

"I hope so," Jessop said. "That's the nicest thing anyone's said to me in a long time."

"Can I suck your tool at the same time while you lick me?" the girl said, noticing Jessop's erection bouncing over his abdomen.

"I wouldn't want you to get distracted from your own pleas–"

But Jessop could barely finish his sentence before the native girl leaned forward, taking his aching erection into her mouth and sucking it like a lollypop. As her hips curled further downward, her clit rolled into his mouth, and he eagerly enveloped it, rolling his tongue over her jewel in slow figure-eights.

"Oh God, yes," the girl huffed. "That feels so good. Don't stop."

Jessop closed his eyes, trying to concentrate on stroking the girl's swelling nub, but when she saw that Jessop didn't have any balls and a dripping pussy in its place, she slid the fingers of one hand deep inside his cavity while she lowered her head further down his throbbing shaft.

"Mhhhh," Jessop groaned in ecstasy. No one had stimulated both of his parts so skillfully before, and he redoubled his efforts to give his partner equal attention.

As the native girl bobbed her head up and down over his swelling shaft, stopping at the top to twirl her tongue around his glans and suck even harder on his crown, he flapped his tongue faster against her burning bulb, trying to match his speed with the pace of her rocking hips. He didn't want to go too fast before she was ready, but he'd learned from his previous encounters with the native women that when they reached the sweet spot in their growing pleasure, it was important not to change the pattern.

"Jessop..." the native girl panted as he twirled his tongue over her engorged glans. "I'm going to come in your mouth. I'm going to come so hard–"

"Mm-hmm," Jessop murmured, feeling his own orgasm budding in his loins while the native girl sucked and jilled him at the same time. It was a different kind of feeling than he was used to, with the first sign of his imminent orgasm normally growing inside his missing balls. The sensation of the girl's fingers stroking the inside of his new pussy created an entirely new sensation, with the walls of his internal cavity tingling just as strongly as throbbing cock. When he felt his pleasure reaching the bursting point, it was as if a tidal wave released over his lower body, and when he began gushing and convulsing at the same time, she groaned loudly, spraying her own juices all over his face, neck and chest as she rocked her hips rapidly over his pursed lips.

The two lovers had been so absorbed in their own pleasure that they'd completely forgotten about their other friends, who suddenly began moaning and panting in simultaneous pleasure. While they watched the foursome shaking their hips against each other's faces in delirious union, Jessop made a mental note from his more recent experience.

It's not always about what's on the outside, he nodded to himself. *Remember to focus just as much on what's on the inside.*

His temporary transformation into a she-male had finally taught him that a woman's erogenous zone extends far deeper than her small outer appendage.

7

———————

Over the next few weeks, the three friends slowly ascended the temple walls, freeing the entombed natives one sculpture at a time while getting in touch with their masculine and feminine sides. It had been an exciting learning experience being temporarily equipped with dual sets of sex organs, and all three of them made the best of their new equipment, experimenting with the tribespeople in ever-expanding ways. When they finally reached the top tier of the temple, they found it surrounded with a single frieze of naked men and women connected hips-to-ass in a continuous chain.

"Now what?" Jessop said, squinting at the long line of fornicating tribespeople. "How are we going to free all of these people at the same time?"

"Maybe we don't have to fuck them one at a time, like with the other sculptures," Clover said. "Since everybody's already connected together this time, maybe we just need to hook up with *one* of them to stimulate the rest of the chain."

"Or *three* of them, in this case," Tara grinned, peering at the buff bodies of the naked tribesmen.

"I dunno," Jessop frowned, squinting more closely at the nature of their connections. "If this involves more *butt*-fucking, I'm not sure I'm up for that again..."

Clover stepped closer to one of the pairings and bent down to examine their genitals.

"I don't think they're doing it that way," she said. "See how they're all paired up man-to-woman? It looks like they're engaging in regular intercourse, albeit from the rear position."

Jessop joined Clover and slid his hand under one of the connected couples, feeling the underside of the woman's buttocks. He could feel the swelling of her labia while her partner probed her pussy with his thick organ.

"Ok," he nodded. "But I don't want to take it from behind from another man, even if it *is* up my pussy. It's not something I've found very enjoyable so far–"

"You haven't tried it with a *ladyboy*, yet," Clover smiled. "There are certain ways to do it that can make it quite satisfying. You've got to have the right angle and the right technique. This is something only a woman would fully understand."

"She's right," Tara said, stepping beside her friends and nodding her head. "If there's one thing I've learned from having both sexual organs this whole time, it's where the most sensitive parts are and what works the best for stimulating each area. Instead of wedging yourself between two native people this time, you could position yourself between Clover and me. We promise to be gentle, plus you can try out some of your new skills on *us* for a change."

"Mm, that does sound interesting," Jessop nodded as his dick started to swell, imagining fucking his friends in ways he'd never tried before. "Shall we finish the job then? This is the last of the natives to be freed."

"It will be kind of sad to see everyone leave," Clover nodded. "But we owe it to the group. Besides, it might be kind of fun to watch everyone coming at the same time. It will be a fitting way to end our adventure at this exotic temple."

"Alright, then," Tara smiled, moving toward one of the couples in the chain. "We only need to break the chain at one point for the three of us to join in. Help me awaken this pair."

Clover and Jessop reaching their hands under the joined hips of the embedded couple, rubbing the tribesman's balls and the sides of the woman's vulva, and before long, the two natives began groaning and rocking their hips while their skin softened and they separated from the wall. The three friends didn't want to interrupt their pleasure, so they waited patiently for the couple to finish their lovemaking, panting and shaking in pleasure as they climaxed together on the edge of the temple.

"Thank you," the native man said when he saw the strange visitors standing beside him. "I don't know how you got here, but we'd never have been freed if it weren't for your kind assistance."

"It's been our pleasure, I assure you," Clover smiled.

"We're intrigued, though," Tara nodded. "We haven't found your *king* anywhere on the temple walls. Some of your colleagues said it was he who trapped you here in stone."

"He's on the inside of the temple," the tribesman said, pointing toward the narrowing peak at the top of the pyramid-shaped structure. "Where nobody can reach him. I suppose he wanted to make sure no one could punish him if we ever became freed."

"Is there a secret passageway into the interior?" Jessop

said, peering upwards. "We haven't seen any doors or portals so far."

"There's a small oculus on the roof of the temple," the tribesman nodded. "But it's a long way down to the bottom. You'd hurt yourself if you tried to enter that way."

"What about on the *outside*, near the base of the building?" Clover asked. "Maybe there's a code or some kind of apparatus to gain access to the inside..."

"Perhaps," the native man said. "But if there is, we have no way of knowing. He closed himself up on the inside before he froze us in punishment for our rebellious behavior."

"We can worry about that later," Tara said, turning toward her friends. "Right now, we've got a few more natives to liberate."

Clover paused as she glanced at the tribesman.

"Do we need to stimulate *each* of your friends to free them all?" she asked.

"I don't think so," he said. "As long as you stimulate one of us sufficiently, your energy will be transmitted through the rest of the chain to wake everyone else up."

"And by *sufficiently*, I'm assuming you mean–?"

"To climax," the man nodded. "That's what it takes to wake us up permanently from our slumber."

"We'll be happy to oblige," Clover smiled, turning toward the quiet native girl who was staring at her tumescent dick. "Why don't you get in front of me while your partner takes the rear position behind Tara? Then Jessop can get in the middle, and if we all come together, hopefully that will wake up the rest of the group."

Jessop hesitated as he squinted his eyes at the narrow gap in the chain created by the newly freed couple.

"How will we all manage to fit in the small space vacated by the newly freed natives?" he said.

"Once the rest of the group starts to come to life and shifts away from the stone," Clover nodded, "you should be able to wedge your way in. Just wait for the right moment, then join in the chain."

"I'm getting used to that," Jessop chuckled. "Slower is sometimes better."

"Exactly," Clover smiled. "You're finally learning."

The pretty native girl positioned herself behind the next man in the locked chain, then Clover slipped in behind her, tilting her hips upward to point her bobbing hard-on toward the girl's still-dripping pussy. The girl reached behind her and inserted Clover's cock into her opening, then she reached under the man in front of her to begin caressing his balls. Meanwhile, the rest of the group watched in amazement as the others in the chain slowly began to move and groan, their stone bodies gradually turning to flesh, one connected pair at a time. By the time their softening skin and shaking bodies stretched all the way around to the other end, Tara nodded at Jessop to get behind Clover's rocking hips while she and the other native man squeezed in behind him. When everyone was finally hooked up, the three friends were joined cock-to-pussy, humping each other's asses while the rest of the chain moaned and rocked their bodies in tandem.

Jessop was enjoying the new feeling of Tara's cock in his pussy, but something felt different this time. He wasn't sure if it was entirely *mental*, knowing he was being fucked by a girl this time, or if it was something about her technique. Whatever it was, he felt an entirely new sensation inside, and as he fucked Clover harder from behind, he began to moan more loudly.

"Whatever you're doing back there," he panted, turning his head halfway around to address Tara. "Don't stop. That feels fantastic."

"I'm stimulating your G-spot," Tara grunted while holding the sides of Jessop's hips to position them in the right direction.

"My *what*?" Jessop said, furrowing his brow.

"It's a spot on the forward surface of your pussy, about two inches inside. That's where the most sensitive tissue is and where a special gland resides that makes women squirt. Try it yourself. Just pull your cock out a few inches and angle your hips downward to stimulate Clover in the same place. I have a feeling she'll like it as much as you are."

Jessop paused as he peered down at Clover's ass and his glistening cock thrusting between her cheeks, then he grabbed the sides of her buttocks and tilted his hips down, feeling the front of her opening tightening around the tip of his tool.

"Yes," Clover panted. "That's the spot, Jess. Fuck me right there. I'm going to gush all over your pussy any second now."

"Holy shit," Jessop grunted, feeling his pleasure escalating from the newfound stimulation of his internal G-spot and the simultaneous squeezing of the glans of his penis by Clover's contracting pussy. I feel like I'm going to explode in a million places–"

"Let it go, baby," Clover huffed in front of him while she angled her hips in kind to stimulate the native girl's own G-spot. "Come all over my pussy and Tara's boy-cock while the rest of these tribespeople reach their promised land. Let's make this last hookup extra special."

"Oh *fuck*," Jessop groaned, feeling his whole body

tensing up and his rapidly approaching orgasm expanding in a way he'd never experienced before. *"Aieeeee..."*

When he finally exploded in a symphony of contractions and convulsions, he felt his dick pulsing hard inside Clover's gushing hole as he simultaneously sprayed his pussy juices backward over Tara's pulsating erection and the tribal man's balls behind her. Before long, the entire chain of connected tribespeople began groaning and shaking their bodies together while holding each other's hips, breasts, and testicles as they savored the longest and sweetest climax they'd ever experienced. By the time everybody finished climaxing, they peered at one another, realizing they'd finally been freed from their eternal bondage and were free to leave the cursed temple that had cast a spell on them for so long. Although Clover, Tara, and Jessop were sorry to see the last of them leave, they were thrilled to have liberated the last of them while enjoying an erotic experience they would never forget.

Now the only matter remaining was to find this mysterious king who'd enslaved his people all this time, and see if the three friends could return to their regular bodies before they left this erotic temple for good.

8

———

"That was *amazing*," Jessop panted, staring down at his still-tingling erection, bobbing up against his heaving abdomen. "Now I think I know everything I need to about how to satisfy a woman. Thanks for sharing that new technique. I've never experienced an orgasm so strong and powerful as that before."

"I'm glad you liked it," Tara smiled. "But I don't think you *ever* stop learning how to please a woman. We're complicated in ways you still haven't deciphered. It's more of a *journey* than a destination."

"A bit like our travels through this strange land of Abbynthia," Clover nodded. "Where will we go next?"

"We still have that little matter of finding these people's leader and teaching him a lesson," Tara said. "I wouldn't mind giving his ass a serious *whupping* if we can get inside this temple."

Jessop nodded, glancing upward toward the last tier of the pyramid where it narrowed to a circle, roughly ten feet in diameter.

"Let's see what we can find by looking through the hole in the top."

The trio climbed up the final level, then peered down through the oculus at the top of the structure, noticing a large figure sitting on the floor of the temple.

"What *is* that, exactly?" Clover said, squinting her eyes at the motionless statue of a large figure sitting with his legs crossed and his hands in his lap.

"It's a man," Tara said. "A very *big* man."

"Is that a–?" Jessop said, widening his eyes.

"A *cock*," Clover nodded, glancing at the huge, upturned pole rising up from his lap. "A very large one."

"And he seems to be rubbing it with his hands," Tara said.

"I wonder if he's been getting off this whole time, listening to us hooking up with his freed tribal members."

"That's kind of sad, if he has," Clover said. "Getting his jollies while his people have been trapped in stone all this time, patiently awaiting their turn to be freed."

"But he's still hard as a *rock*," Jessop said, staring at the motionless figure. "If you'll pardon the pun."

"I wonder if we can free him the same way as the others," Tara said.

"Should we even *try*?" Clover said, wrinkling her brow in disapproval. "Maybe we should leave him locked in there for eternity, like the rest of his tribespeople that he froze to the walls of his temple."

"Although he *did* leave an opening for them to be freed," Tara said. "He knew if they were ever discovered by outsiders that they could eventually be freed from their bondage. Plus, we still have these bisexual *organs* to deal with. Maybe he's the only one who can end the spell..."

"Are you sure you *want* to?" Clover smiled at her friend.

"You have to admit, it's been kind of fun, alternating the role of man and woman at our pleasure."

"And there's been a *lot* of pleasure involved in the process," Jessop grinned.

"Are you happy running around without your balls for the *rest of time*?" Tara said, peering down at Jessop's pink slit where he used to have a scrotum. "As much as you may be enjoying getting in touch with your feminine side while you're equipped with your little boy-pussy, are you sure you want everyone to see you emasculated this way?"

"Okay, if you put it *that* way..." Jessop frowned.

Tara paused as she peered through the oculus toward the top of the king's bald head, more than fifty feet below.

"It's too far down to jump from here," she said. "And there doesn't seem to be any footholds or indentations in the walls to crawl down with. I think the only way in will be from the outside."

"But we didn't notice any other portals on the way up," Clover said. "Maybe if we search more thoroughly on the ground level, we can find some kind of entrance."

"We better get started soon," Jessop said, glancing at the long shadows stretching over the courtyard surrounding the temple from the tall trees at the edge of the forest. "It will get dark soon, making it harder to search for clues."

"Jessop's right," Tara nodded. "We're not quite finished here yet."

～

The three friends climbed down from the top of the temple, then slowly began walking around the base of the structure, now devoid of any last vestige of naked tribespeople. They were looking for something unusual, like a lever or a handle that might move the heavy stones and give them access to the interior. About halfway around the building, they stopped in front of an unusual carving they'd given little attention to previously. It depicted two tall tribesmen wearing warrior costumes, holding crossed spears over what appeared to be an intricately carved large door.

"How did we miss *this* one before?" Clover said, peering at the steely expressions of the frozen effigies.

"We were too busy concentrating on the naked figures of the *other* tribespeople," Tara chuckled. "These guys don't look like they're in any mood for fun and games."

"And besides," Jessop nodded. "How could we wake them from their frozen slumber without access to their sex organs? They're completely covered in heavy armor."

"Well, not *completely*," Clover said, moving forward a few steps and caressing the bare legs of one of the guards beneath his pleated leather skirt.

The effigy began to rumble and within a few minutes, the front of his skirt slowly began to rise, revealing a thick, upturned cock under his loosening garment.

"See?" Clover said excitedly to Tara. "You try the other one. These guys are probably *dying* to get off after being locked up in stone all this time."

Tara quickly stepped forward and repeated the procedure with the other guard, and sure enough, both of the guards soon began to shake and turn to flesh as their skin softened and they stepped away from the wall.

"Who goes there?" one of the guards said, staring at the newcomers in surprise.

"No one's permitted to enter this temple!" the other guard grunted, equally defiant.

"Come now," Clover smiled, staring at their throbbing

erections, bobbing up under their Roman-style battle skirts and bronze breastplates. "Surely you don't want to stand here forever frozen in stone, guarding this abandoned temple?"

The two guards peered upwards, then their eyes widened at the sight of the temple's now bare walls, furrowing their brows in confusion.

"How did you–?" the first one said, staring at the trio's strange bodies.

"The same way we brought *you* two to life," Tara grinned, noticing their dicks remaining as firm and pointed as their upturned spears. "By sucking and fucking each of them until they climaxed like they haven't done in decades."

"You shouldn't have done that," the second guard huffed. "Our king wouldn't approve–"

"Wasn't he the one who cast the spell that put all of you in stone in the first place?" Clover said. "He wouldn't have allowed them to be freed in this manner if that wasn't also part of the plan."

The guards peered at one another for a moment, furrowing their brows while they contemplated what to do with these strange new visitors.

"I know what you're thinking," Tara smiled, staring at their fluttering skirts while she grasped the base of her dick, waving it around. "But your *little* heads seem to be thinking something else. Wouldn't you like a piece of this and experience some *pleasure* for a change of pace?"

"I don't know–" the first guard muttered.

"Fuck it," the second guard said, throwing down his spear. "I've stayed locked up here long enough. There's no reason to guard the temple any longer with all of our people gone. The king can fend for himself from now on."

Tara stepped forward and knelt down in front of the

guard, lifting his skirt over his waist while taking his throbbing cock into her mouth.

"Mmm," she murmured. "You taste good. I bet you've got a lot of spunk stored up that you're just dying to shoot down my throat–"

"Oh, fuck," the guardsman moaned, grabbing hold of Tara's head and pulling her mouth deeper over his swelling tool. "I've missed this so much..."

"See?" Clover said, smiling at the first guard while she swung her tool teasingly between her legs. "Wouldn't like some of that also? Or perhaps you'd like a *different* piece of me? We're happy to please."

"Oh my God," the guard said, staring at Clover's bobbing ladyboy cock.

She stepped onto the ledge where he was standing then she hopped up over his hips, wrapping her legs around his waist. The guard lifted the bottom of his skirt and pointed his erection into her dripping opening, then he groaned in intense pleasure as he stared down at her cock rubbing up against his stomach.

While Jessop stood a few feet further away watching his friends servicing the two guards, he inspected the heavy door for any sign of an opening. The louder the guardsmen moaned and the faster their hips rocked against Clover's and Tara's bodies, the more the door shook, until it suddenly swung open when the guards emptied their loads deep into the women's cavities.

"Thanks," Tara said, pulling her head off the second guardsman's dripping dick and wiping the side of her face.

"No," the first guardsman smiled, lifting Clover off his bobbing hard-on. "Thank *you*. You're the ones who've done us a favor. *All* of us."

"Think nothing of it," Clover said. "We enjoyed it just as much as the rest of you."

"Where will you go now?" Jessop said to the two guardsmen, eager to make sure they'd no longer be an impediment to their further exploration of the temple.

"As far from this place as we possibly *can*," the first guard said, nodding toward his colleague. "I've had plenty enough time locked in limbo without exercising my natural impulses. What do you say, Ragnar? Are you ready to leave this god-forsaken place?"

"Damn right," the second guardsman said. "We've got a lot of catching up to do."

9

———

After the two guards left the palace, the three friends entered through the half-open door, peering inside the eerie structure, still lit partially from above by the overhead sun.

"It's quiet as a ghost in here," Clover said, peering up at the giant statue of the sitting Buddha-king.

"Yeah," Tara said, glancing at the bare interior walls of the building. "It looks like he's had this place all to himself all this time."

"Poor guy," Jessop nodded, glancing at the king's hands wrapped around the base of his upturned phallus. "It looks like he's had to satisfy himself with all of his people locked on the outside."

"I wouldn't feel *too* sorry for him," Clover chuckled, noticing his marble erection extending all the way up toward his lips. "With a cock *that* big, his pleasure must be equally intense."

"Yes," Jessop smiled. "Especially if he can *suck* it at the same time."

"Not when he's frozen in *stone*," Tara said. "Should we try to see if we can free him from his suspended animation?"

"How will we do that, exactly?" Clover said, glancing at the king's enormous balls resting at the base of his upturned organ. "We'd barely be able to get our arms around that thing, let alone our pussies."

"Maybe our *legs* could fit, though," Tara nodded, wrinkling her forehead in thought. "If we could shimmy up to the tip of his tool and concentrate our attention on his swelling *glans*, that might be enough to stimulate him out of his slumber."

"All *three* of us?" Jessop said.

"Why don't you stay at the bottom and stimulate his *balls* at the same time?" Tara said. "The more ways we can stimulate him, the faster we might awaken him."

"I'll try," Jessop said, shaking his head at how he'd play with the king's testicles when each of them was almost as big as his entire body.

"Good," Tara said, peering toward Clover as she pondered how to climb the king's towering pole. "We'll need to link our hands to climb our way up this guy's giant erection."

"Just try to keep your *fantasies* in check while we do it," Clover chuckled. "It'll be a lot more slippery if we're dripping juices out of our pussy at the same time."

"We'll save that for the top," Tara nodded. "Keep your dick in your pants until we get there."

"I would if I still had them *with* me," Clover smiled. "I seem to have left them on the other side of the temple when we began fucking the naked natives."

"Come on," Tara said, grabbing Clover's hand. "Maybe our sticky bodies will work to our advantage as we try to scale this smooth marble. Just make sure you hold on tight so we don't fall."

The two friends walked up to the base of the motionless king's thick erection, standing on top of his balls while they stared upward toward the overhead light shining on his glistening tip.

"I think he's already starting to get excited," Tara said to Clover. "Are you ready?"

"Ready as I'll ever be," Clover nodded.

They wrapped their arms around the wide circumference of the marble phallus, then they interlocked their fingers as they curled their legs around the big pole, gripping it as tightly as they could with their muscles.

"Ooomph," Clover grunted, shifting her hips upward a few inches as the two women moved their hands higher.

"It's working," Tara huffed, tensing her leg muscles against the hard phallus.

"Yeah," Clover grunted. "Only another couple hundred feet to go..."

The two women continued shimmying their bodies up the shiny pole a few feet at a time until they finally reached the top of the king's thick organ. Then they scurried on top of his smooth crown to catch their breath, sliding their fingers gently over the slit in his glans that was as big as a woman's vulva.

"Look," Tara said, lifting her hand as a sticky string of liquid dripped from her fingers. "He's already beginning to get turned on!"

"Okay," Clover nodded, rubbing his pre-cum over the surface of his softening glans. "But how will we get him fully aroused? I'm not sure this will be enough stimulation to give him a full orgasm."

Tara glanced the long way down toward the base of the temple at Jessop, who appeared hardly bigger than an ant sitting on the king's enormous testicles.

"How are you doing down there, Jessop?" she yelled. "Are you noticing any rumbling in the king's balls?"

"Not yet," Jessop yelled back. "But I think maybe they're beginning to soften up somewhat. How are you doing up top?"

"We're still trying to figure out how to jerk this guy's dick without falling off," Clover chuckled. "Keep stimulating his scrotum while we massage his not-so-little head."

"I've got an idea," Tara said, sliding one of her hands further down the king's dripping glans, under the sensitive curvature of his frenulum. "If we interlock our legs around the base of his corona where it narrows partially, we might be able to stimulate him in his most sensitive place to bring him back to life."

"Okay," Clover said, squinting at Tara with narrowed eyes. "But what will we do if he *comes*? All of that slippery liquid will make us lose our grip, and it's a long way down."

"We'll face that possibility when it arrives," Tara chuckled. "Hopefully he'll catch us with his hands when he awakens."

"If he doesn't *crush* us first."

"Just keep your wits about you, and concentrate on the task at hand. Or perhaps I should say, at *foot*."

"Very funny," Clover smiled, glancing at her friend with a lopsided grin.

"Okay," Tara said, holding out her arms toward Clover. "Grip my hands while we lower our hips over the base of his helmet."

The two girls interlaced their fingers tightly together,

then they slowly lowered their bodies over the king's swelling corona, wrapping their legs around his throbbing frenulum.

"Now what?" Clover said, staring at the king's darkening skin while she held on for dear life.

"His skin is beginning to change color, like more blood is flowing to this part of his cock," Tara said. "I think we need to find a way to rub his dick more *firmly* to arouse him fully."

"How do you propose we do that, with our legs surrounding him like a *tourniquet*?"

"Use your *hands* to grip the upper part of his crown while we twist our hips to slide our legs around his underside."

"That's easy for *you* to say," Clover grunted, trying to shift her body as Tara instructed.

"Yes!" Tara shouted, feeling the hard marble of the king's phallus beginning to soften and turn to flesh. "Just like that. I don't think it will take too much more to do the trick. He's already starting to awaken."

"Okay," Clover said, beginning to feel her hands losing their grip as the king's slit began to drip more pre-cum over the top of his organ. "But it's getting harder to hold on–"

"Just a little longer," Tara said, digging her fingers into the softening flesh and twisting her body harder around his swelling glans. "I can feel him shaking..."

Clover glanced at the surface of the king's trembling erection, widening her eyes as she saw it begin to crack and crumble.

"Are you sure that's *shaking*?" she said. "It looks more like crumbling. I'm not sure we're bringing him to life so much as giving him a slow *death*."

"I fear you might be right," Tara said, noticing long

cracks forming in the king's upturned pole, with large chunks of skin falling down overtop of Jessop.

"What are you guys doing down up there?" he yelled, quickly scrambling down from the king's quaking testicles while he took cover.

"We're not exactly sure," Tara said, gripping the base of the king's glans more tightly with her legs as she tried to hold on to the shaking and crumbling phallus.

"I think it might be time to abandon this idea," Clover yelled, feeling the torrent of sticky juices rolling over her head and shoulders from the king's quivering cock.

"I think you're right," Tara nodded, loosening her grip on the king's swelling glans. "Let's use his lubrication to our advantage. Ease your grip on his dick and slide down this pole with me."

The two friends loosened their grip on the upper surface of the king's crown, then they relaxed their legs just enough to begin sliding down the pole. As they started falling, the enormous phallus shook harder and harder, dropping huge chunks of flesh and stone all around them, until they bounced over his tightening balls at the base of his dick and grabbed Jessop's hands, rushing out the entrance of the temple, which had begun slowly closing. They barely managed to slip out the opening before they heard an enormous crash and saw a giant geyser of liquid shooting out the opening of the oculus, then the entire temple crumbled and fell to the ground, leaving nothing but a choking pile of dust.

"Holy shit," Clover huffed, waving her hand in front of her face to clear the settling dust. "We barely made it out of there alive!"

"Yeah," Tara nodded, glancing around her at the giant

puddle of splooge the king had ejected in the final throes of his deafening climax. "It looks like the king got his just reward, after all."

Jessop suddenly felt a strange tingling in his hips, and he peered down between his legs.

"That's not the *only* thing that's changed," he said. As he rolled his hands over the base of his cock, he felt his familiar scrotum back in place of his previous girl-pussy. "I'm back to being a full-blown *man* again."

The two girls glanced at his balls, then peered down at their own crotches, noticing their penises shriveling and disappearing between their legs, replaced with the small pink pea of their clits, gleaming proudly at the junction of their dripping slits in the settling sun.

"Wow," Tara nodded. "I guess that was all it took to shake the spell he put on us. Free all of his people and give him one last giant orgasm to eliminate any sign of this lost tribe in the forest forever."

"I'm going to miss my boy-cock," Clover said, rubbing her tingling button to make sure it still worked. "But I'm kind of glad I've got my old body back. That was kind of weird, having a big dick sticking out from my pussy."

"Don't worry," Jessop smiled, his own swelling organ beginning to rise once again over his hips as he felt the familiar tingling in his balls from a renewed sense of arousal watching his friends playing with their old pussies. "We've still got *one* good cock to share between us. And I've learned a few tricks from being around all these kinky tribespeople regarding how to use it."

"I bet you have," Tara chuckled, watching Jessop bat his hard-on from side to side while he squeezed his new balls tightly. "So have *we*."

R eady *for more erotic chills and thrills? Read the next volume in Clover's Fantasy Adventures: The Magic Pool. Buy direct and save at victoriarusherotica. Or download from your favorite online bookstore here: retailer links.*

This hot spring stimulates a lot more than just your muscles...

ALSO BY VICTORIA RUSH

Adult Fairytales:

The Enchanted Forest: An Erotic Fairytale

The Land of Giants: An Erotic Fairytale

The Dragon's Lair: An Erotic Fairytale

Witch's Brew: An Erotic Fairytale

The Mage's Spell: An Erotic Fairytale

The Mermaid Lagoon: An Erotic Fairytale

The Coven: An Erotic Fairytale

Rapunzel: An Erotic Fairytale

The Seven Dwarfs: An Erotic Fairytale

The Land of Mutants: An Erotic Fairytale

The Erotic Temple: A Sexy Fairytale (Coming Soon)

Erotica Themed Bundles:

Voyeur: Lesbian Erotica Bundle

Public Affairs: A Lesbian Anthology

Futa Fantasies: The Ladyboy Collection

Threesomes: The Lesbian Collection

Threesomes - Volume 2: The Lesbian Collection

First Time: A Lesbian Anthology

Hedonism: An Erotic Anthology

Switch Hitters: Bisexual Erotica

Taboo Erotica: The Lesbian Series

BDSM: The Lesbian Collection

Party Games: The Erotic Collection

Party Games 2: The Erotic Collection

All Girl 1: Lesbian Erotica Bundle

All Girl 2: Lesbian Erotica Bundle

All Girl 3: Lesbian Erotica Bundle

All Girl 4: Lesbian Erotica Bundle

Erotic Fairytale Bundles:

Clover's Fantasy Adventures: Books 1 - 5

Clover's Fantasy Adventures: Books 6 - 10

Erotic Fantasy:

Pirate's Bounty: A Time Travel Adventure

Wild West: A Time Travel Adventure

Private Riley: A Time Travel Adventure

Cleopatra's Secret: A Time Travel Adventure

Bounty Hunter 2125: A Time Travel Adventure

Ninja Assassin: A Time Travel Adventure

The 300: A Time Travel Adventure

Arabian Nights: An Erotic Fairytale (coming soon...)

Steamy Time Travel Bundles:

Riley's Time Travel Adventures: Books 1 - 5

Lesbian Erotica:

The Dinner Party: Lesbian Voyeur Erotica

The Darkroom: Bisexual Voyeur Erotica

Naked Yoga: Lesbian Transgender Erotica

Nude Cruise: Bisexual Voyeur Erotica

Rush Hour: Taboo Public Sex

The Girl Next Door: First Time Lesbian Erotic Romance

Girls' Camp: Lesbian Group Sex

Wet Dream: Ladyboy Fantasy Erotica

The Convent: Taboo Sex with a Nun

Sex Robot: A Dream Sex Machine

The Personal Trainer: Getting Pumped at the Gym

The Dominatrix: BDSM Lesbian Domination

Webcam Chat: Lesbian Online Sex

Paint Me: A Kinky Bodypainting Workshop

The Toy Party: Girls Sharing Sex Toys

The Costume Party: Strapping One On

Swedish Sauna: Lesbian Group Sex

The Therapist: Taboo Lesbian Erotica

Elevator Shaft: Bisexual Threesomes Erotica

Ladyboy: Lesbian Transgender Erotica

Peep Show: Lesbian Voyeur Erotica

The Dare: Public Sex Erotica

Maid Service: Lesbian Threesomes Erotica

The Hitchhiker: First Time Lesbian Erotica

The Housesitter: Spycam Lesbian Erotica

The Spa: Lesbian Group Orgy

Parlor Games: Blindfold Sex Party

The Exchange Student: First Time Lesbian Erotica

The Hostel: Bisexual Group Erotica

The Harem: Lesbian Erotic Romance

The Orient Express: Lesbian Voyeur Erotica

The First Lady: A Forbidden Lesbian Erotic Romance

The Slave: Lesbian BDSM Erotica

The Masseuse: Lesbian Sensuous Erotica

Too Close for Comfort: Lesbian Forbidden Erotica

Naked Twister: A Wild Party Game

Lexi: The Sex App (Lesbian Fantasy Erotica)

Call Girl: Lesbian Bisexual Threesomes Erotica

Circle Jill: Lesbian Masturbation Workshop

The Viewing Room: Masturbation Voyeur Erotica

Spin the Bottle: A Kinky Party Game

The Hair Salon: Lesbian Voyeur Erotica

Tribadism 1: Girls Only Sex Workshop

Tribadism 2: The Art of Scissoring

Tribadism 3: Threeway Hookups

The Kiss: A Game of Oral Sex

Pledge Week: Sorority Sisters

Carny Games 1: A Wild Sex Party

Carny Games 2: A Kinky Sex Party

Carny Games 3: An Erotic Sex Party

Dreamscape: An Artificial Reality Game

Glory Hole: Guess Who's On the Other Side

Joy Ride: A Late Night Erotic Bus Trip

The Blind Girl: An Erotic Romance(Coming Soon)

Lesbian Erotica Bundles:

Jade's Erotic Adventures: Books 1 - 5

Jade's Erotic Adventures: Books 6 - 10

Jade's Erotic Adventures: Books 11 - 15

Jade's Erotic Adventures: Books 16 - 20

Jade's Erotic Adventures: Books 21 - 25

Jade's Erotic Adventures: Books 26 - 30

Jade's Erotic Adventures: Books 31 - 35

Jade's Erotic Adventures: Books 36 - 40

Jade's Erotic Adventures: Books 41 - 45

Jade's Erotic Adventures: Books 46 - 50

Fifty Shades of Jade: Superbundle

Standalone Stories:

The Polynesian Girl: A Lesbian EroticRomance

FOLLOW VICTORIA RUSH:

Want to keep informed of my latest erotic book releases? Sign up for my newsletter and receive a FREE bonus book:

Spying on the neighbors just got a lot more interesting...